# The Gingerbread Man

Told by Nancy Nolte

Illustrated by RICHARD SCARRY

g A GOLDEN BOOK • NEW YORK

Copyright © 1953, renewed 1981 by Random House, Inc. All rights reserved under International and Pan-American Copyright Conventions. Published in the United States by Golden Books, an imprint of Random House Children's Books, a division of Random House, Inc., New York, and simultaneously in Canada by Random House of Canada Limited, Toronto. Originally published in 1953 in slightly different form by Simon and Schuster, Inc., and Artists and Writers Guild, Inc. Golden Books, A Golden Book, Big Little Golden Book, the G colophon, and the distinctive gold spine are registered trademarks of Random House, Inc. Library of Congress Control Number: 2002114233
ISBN 0-375-82589-4 (trade) — ISBN 0-375-92589-9 (lib. bdg.)
www.goldenbooks.com
Printed in Malaysia        First Random House Edition 2004
10 9 8 7 6 5

Visit us on the Web! www.randomhouse.com/kids
Educators and librarians, for a variety of teaching tools, visit us at
www.randomhouse.com/teachers

Once upon a time a little old man and a little old woman lived in a neat little house in a wood.

Every day the little old woman baked wonderful
cookies and cakes and pies for the little old man. One
day she decided to bake something special for him.

So she made a beautiful gingerbread man! He had raisins for eyes, a currant for his nose, and a pink sugar-candy waistcoat.

She popped him into the oven to bake.

When he was done, the little old woman took him out of the oven, laid him on the table to cool, and went out in the yard to water the flowers.

As soon as she was out of sight, the gingerbread
man sat up on the table. Seeing that no one was
around, he climbed down and ran out the door
and away down the path.

The little old woman saw him.

"Stop! Stop!" she cried.

And she started to run after him.

But the gingerbread man only laughed over his shoulder and called:

"Run, run as fast as you can.

You can't catch me—

I'm the Gingerbread Man!"

And with that he ran even faster, with the little old woman running behind him.

Soon they came to the field where the little old man was busy planting cabbages. When he saw the gingerbread man running away and the little old woman trying to stop him, he cried out, "Stop! Stop!"

But the gingerbread man only laughed and called back:

"Run, run as fast as you can.

You can't catch me—

I'm the Gingerbread Man!

I got away from the little old woman

And I can get away from you,

I can, I can."

And with that he ran even faster, with the little old woman and the little old man running as fast as they could behind him.

Soon he came to a pasture where a gentle brown cow was chewing her cud. When the cow saw the delicious gingerbread man running down the road, she thought of how good he would taste, so she cried, "Stop! Stop!"

But the gingerbread man only laughed and called back:

"Run, run as fast as you can.

You can't catch me—

I'm the Gingerbread Man!

I got away from the little old woman and
   the little old man,

And I can get away from you,

I can, I can."

And with that he ran even faster, with the little old woman, the little old man, and the gentle brown cow after him.

The gingerbread man was getting tired now, but he would not give up.

Then he saw a big brown bear eating honey from a tree, and he knew that he would have to run even faster.

When the bear smelled the wonderful gingery smell, he thought how good the gingerbread man would taste with his honey. So the bear cried, "Stop! Stop!"

But the gingerbread man drew a deep breath and laughed and cried out:

"Run, run as fast as you can.

You can't catch me—

I'm the Gingerbread Man!

I got away from the little old woman,

   the little old man, and the gentle brown cow,

And I can get away from you,

I can, I can."

And on he ran, with the little old woman, the little old man, the gentle brown cow, and the big brown bear all running after him.

At last the gingerbread man saw a river before him and he did not know how he could cross it. But a wily red fox was sitting near the river, and when he saw the gingerbread man, he decided that he would eat him.

As the gingerbread man ran up to the river's edge, the wily red fox came out to meet him.

"Jump on my tail and I will carry you across the river," he called to the gingerbread man.

"If I do, you will eat me," said the gingerbread man.

"Oh, no!" declared the fox. "I don't like gingerbread."

So the gingerbread man jumped on the fox's
tail, and the fox waded into the river.

But soon the water grew so deep that it lapped
about the toes of the little gingerbread man.

"Fox!" he said. "I am getting wet."

"Jump on my back!" cried the wily red fox.

The gingerbread man jumped on the fox's back, but again the water started to lap about the gingerbread man's feet.

"Fox!" he said again. "I am getting wet."

"Jump on my head," cried the fox.
The gingerbread man jumped to the fox's head, but the water soon crept up.

"Jump on my nose," said the wily red fox.
The gingerbread man jumped onto the fox's
nose and—snip! snip! the fox gobbled him up!

And that is just what should happen to all gingerbread men!